The Saddest Pony

Do you love ponies? Be a Pony Pal!

PONY PALS

The Saddest Pony

Jeanne Betancourt

illustrated by Vivien Kubbos

SCHOLASTIC INC.
New York Toronto London Auckland Sydney
Mexico City New Delhi Hong Kong

ISBN 0-590-51295-1

12 11 10 9 8 7 6   0 1/0 2/0

Printed in the U.S.A.   40

First Scholastic printing, November 1998
Cover and text illustrations by Vivien Kubbos
Typeset in Bookman

Contents

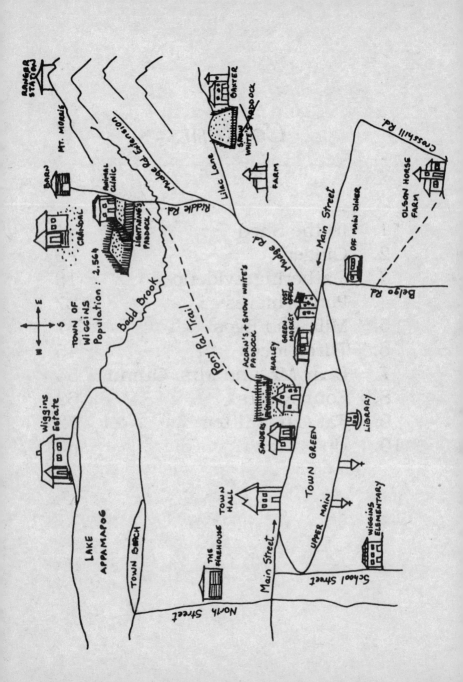

In the Shed

It was a sunny morning in Wiggins. Pam Crandal rode her pony, Lightning, alone on Riddle Road. Later, she would meet her Pony Pals, Anna and Lulu, for a picnic.

Pam turned Lightning onto Mudge Road Extension. "We haven't ridden out here in a long time," she told her pony. Lightning agreed with a nod.

Pam trotted and then galloped Lightning along the deserted road. When she slowed her pony down to a walk, Lightning suddenly stopped. Her ears flickered back and forth.

Pam listened, wondering what had stopped Lightning. Birds chirped in the trees above them. Lightning turned her head. She wasn't listening to the birds. She was hearing something Pam couldn't hear.

Lightning walked towards a dirt driveway, snorted and nodded her head. Pam tugged on the reins to move her back onto the road. "We don't have time to explore," she told Lightning. But Lightning still wanted to go up the rutted driveway. She nickered as if to say, "Let's go this way."

Pam decided to let the pony follow her curiosity.

The dirt driveway ended near an old, run-down farmhouse. Pam also saw a barn without a roof and a small horse shed.

"I don't think anyone lives here anymore," Pam told Lightning. She tried to turn Lightning around.

Lightning whinnied and pulled towards the horse shed. Pam heard another pony's whinny answer Lightning's.

"So that's what you heard before!"

exclaimed Pam. "A pony's in there! But we can't visit the pony, Lightning. We haven't been invited."

Lightning whinnied towards the shed again. The pony in the shed whinnied back. Pam thought the pony's whinny sounded weak and a little strange. Was something wrong with that pony?

Pam decided to investigate.

She looked towards the house. She saw a rusty, old truck with a wheel missing, but there was no sign of a car or any activity.

"Okay, Lightning," she said softly. "Let's go see this pony."

Pam led Lightning around the shed. She heard a nicker before she saw the pony's head hanging out the shed door.

The pony watched Pam and Lightning come towards her. Pam thought the pony had the saddest eyes she had ever seen.

"Hello, pony," said Pam. She stroked the pony's matted, dirty mane. Lightning wanted to say hello to the pony, too. But Pam was afraid the pony might be sick. She

didn't want Lightning to catch a disease. So she tied Lightning to a fence post.

Pam looked at the pony's body through the shed door. Her coat was matted and dirty. The stall was filthy, too. And the pony was very skinny. She looked terrible. She looked neglected.

"Poor pony," said Pam sadly. "Doesn't anybody take care of you?"

The pony nuzzled Pam's shoulder. Pam gave her head a little hug.

Lightning whinnied. Pam turned. Lightning's ears flickered back again. Pam stood still and listened carefully. She heard the sound of voices coming from the direction of the old house.

Pam quickly untied Lightning. She looked around for a way to leave without being seen. "This way, Lightning," she whispered. She led her pony behind the barn, across the field and into the woods.

When they reached Mudge Road Extension, Pam mounted Lightning and galloped towards Pony Pal Trail. Anna and

Lulu would be waiting for her there. Pony Pal Trail was a mile-and-a-half horse path through the woods. It connected Pam's place to Anna's and Lulu's. Pam couldn't wait to tell her friends about the pitiful pony Lightning had discovered.

Anna and Lulu and their ponies, Acorn and Snow White, were waiting for Pam and Lightning at three birch trees. Lightning whinnied happily. Snow White nodded her head and Acorn nickered hello. The ponies liked one another. They were Pony Pals, too.

The three ponies and riders stood in a circle.

"Pam, we packed the best lunch," said Anna. "Ham and cheese sandwiches and, of course, brownies."

"Let's go to our favorite spot on Badd Brook and eat now," said Lulu.

"There's something I have to tell you first," said Pam.

"What?" asked Lulu.

"You look upset, Pam," observed Anna.

"Lightning found a neglected pony," said Pam. "Off Mudge Road Extension."

Pam told her friends all about the sad pony.

"We have to do something to help that pony," said Anna.

"Can we go see her?" asked Lulu.

"Okay," agreed Pam. "I'll take you there."

"We can eat later," added Anna.

Pam and Lightning took the lead. The Pony Pals rode along Pony Pal Trail, galloped across the Crandals' big field, and trotted along Mudge Road Extension until they saw the rutted driveway.

"I'll stay in the woods with our ponies," said Pam. "You go look. But be careful. Don't let anyone see you."

Lightning wanted to go with Anna and Lulu, but Pam held her lead tightly. "You stay with me," she told her pony. "But don't worry, we'll find a way to help the sad pony."

Pam was nervous in the woods while Anna and Lulu were gone. She thought, anyone who doesn't take care of their pony wouldn't be nice to people either. What if the pony's owner caught them?

In a few minutes, Pam saw Anna and Lulu running towards her. They were out of breath. "What happened?" asked Pam.

"Someone came into the shed," said Anna breathlessly.

"I'm glad we weren't inside," said Lulu. "We ducked out of sight just in time."

"But we saw the pony," said Anna. "She was so thin."

"And unhappy," said Lulu.

"I think she's the saddest pony I've ever seen," whispered Anna. There were tears in Anna's eyes.

"I know," said Pam. "We have to do something to help her."

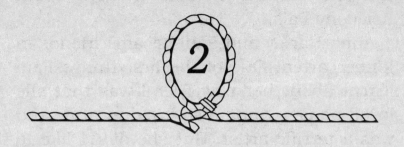

Ginger

The Pony Pals led their ponies back to Mudge Road Extension. "Let's have our picnic in Morristown," suggested Lulu. "And talk about the pony."

Morristown was a ghost town near Mudge Road Extension. No one had lived there in over a hundred years. There were good riding trails and interesting ruins in Morristown.

"I'll lead the way," said Lulu.

"And I'll go last," said Pam.

As the three girls rode along the trail

towards Morristown, Pam thought about her Pony Pals.

Anna Harley and Pam became friends in kindergarten. One of the first things Pam learnt about her new friend was that she loved ponies. Anna also loved to draw and was a terrific artist. But she didn't like to read or do school work nearly as much as Pam did. Pam loved school and always had the best grades. Anna and Pam still had a lot in common. They both loved to be outside having adventures, especially with their ponies.

Lulu Sanders loved nature and ponies, too. Lulu's mother died when she was little. Her father was a writer who studied wild animals. After Lulu's mother died, Lulu often traveled to faraway places with her father. But when Lulu turned ten, Mr. Sanders decided she should live in one place. So Lulu moved in with her Grandmother Sanders on Main Street in Wiggins. Lulu's grandmother had a beauty parlor in the front of her house. The house was next door to Anna's house. Lulu and Anna became friends, and Acorn and Snow White became stable mates.

Lightning had many stable mates. Pam's mother was a riding teacher. The Crandals had three ponies and several horses that belonged to Mrs. Crandal's riding school. Pam's father was a veterinarian. His clinic was next to the Crandals' house. Pam loved having so many animals in her life.

Anna and Lulu loved ponies as much as Pam did. Pam knew she could count on her Pony Pals to help the poor pony.

Pam pulled Lightning to a stop near a stone wall. The girls tied their ponies to trees and gave them each an apple. Then they sat on the stone wall to eat their picnic.

"Who owns that pony?" Anna asked.

"I don't know," said Pam. "I didn't even know there was a farm back there until today."

"I didn't see any other animals," said Lulu.

"And no crops," noted Pam.

"The whole place looked really run down," added Anna.

"Does someone live in that house?" asked Lulu.

"I *did* hear voices," said Pam.

"What can we do for that poor pony?" wondered Anna.

"I think we should investigate . . ." said Lulu. "And gather evidence. That will help us decide what to do."

Pam put their sandwich wrappers in the lunch bag. "I have my binoculars with me," she said. "We can use them to spy."

"And I have my drawing pad," added Anna.

"Great," said Pam. "Let's draw a map of the property right now. We can plan our investigation."

Anna went over to Acorn and took her pad and drawing pencil out of her saddle bag. She sat on the stone wall between Pam and Lulu and made a map.

Pam drew a row of arrows through the

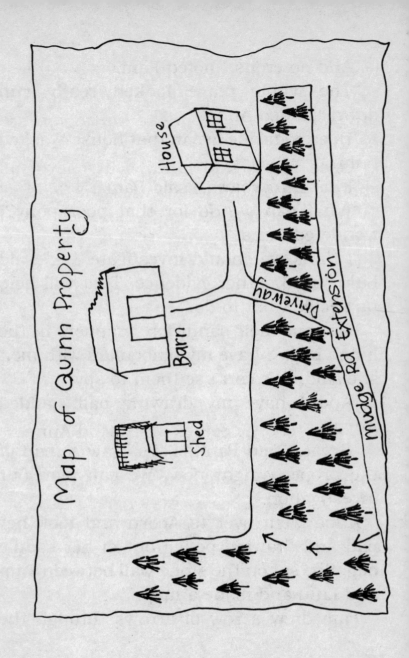

woods. "Let's go through the woods over here," she said, "instead of up the driveway. No one from the house can see us there."

"Good idea," said Lulu. "But one of us should stay in the woods with our ponies."

"The other two can go to the shed," said Anna. "One be a lookout while the other investigates."

"The lookout person can use binoculars," said Lulu.

"Let's go," said Pam.

The Pony Pals rode back to Mudge Road Extension. They got off their ponies and led them through the woods.

"I'll watch our ponies first," said Anna.

Pam patted Lightning on the neck. "We're going to try to help your new friend," she said. "But you have to stay here."

Lulu and Pam headed across the field. They were halfway to the shed when Pam thought she heard a voice. "Quick," she whispered to Lulu. "Over here."

The two girls ducked behind a clump of

bushes.

Pam heard banging in the shed and then the pony's sad whinny. That is the sound of a sick pony, thought Pam.

"Ginger. Ginger. You are a bad old girl," yelled an old man's voice.

Lulu and Pam exchanged a worried glance. Was the man hitting the pony?

A few minutes later the man came out of the shed. Pam raised the binoculars to her face. She could only see his back. He walked slowly towards the house. Pam noticed that he used a cane and there were holes in his sweater.

The side door to the house opened. An old woman came out to meet the man. They went into the house together. The door banged closed.

"All clear," Pam told Lulu.

"I'll be the first lookout," said Lulu.

"Okay," Pam said. She handed Lulu the binoculars.

The two girls, staying low, ran the rest of the way to the shed. Pam wondered what they would find inside.

Had the man hurt the pony named Ginger? Was Ginger an abused pony?

3

Gathering Evidence

Pam opened the shed door and went in. It was dark and smelly inside.

"Hi, Ginger," Pam said softly. "I'm here to help you."

Ginger whinnied a weak hello.

Pam ran her hand along Ginger's side. She could feel her ribs through the hair. A big clump of winter coat came off in Pam's hand.

Pam's eyes were getting used to the dim light. She lifted Ginger's front foot and inspected her hoof.

Next Pam looked around the shed. She noticed a tipped-over water bucket. Ginger lowered her head and pushed the bucket with her nose. She nickered as if to say, "I'm thirsty."

Pam picked up the empty bucket. "I'll fill it for you," she said.

Pam slipped out of the shed and walked around until she found a faucet on the side of the shed. She filled the bucket with water.

Lulu was keeping her lookout from behind a big tree. She watched the house through Pam's binoculars.

Pam snapped her fingers to get Lulu's attention. "Lulu," Pam called. "I'll be the lookout now. You bring this water to Ginger."

Pam and Lulu changed places. Lulu went into the shed with the bucket of water.

A few minutes later Lulu came back to the tree. "Ginger drank a lot of water," she whispered.

"Good," said Pam. "I'll go watch our

ponies so Anna can investigate." She handed the binoculars back to Lulu.

While Pam watched the three ponies, she wrote notes about Ginger. Lightning sniffed at Pam's jacket and nickered.

"You smell Ginger," said Pam. She rubbed her hand along Lightning's side. Lightning's body was strong and firm. Pam remembered Ginger's bony side. "Poor Ginger," Pam told Lightning. "She needs a lot of help."

The girls were quiet during the ride back to Pam's. They were thinking about Ginger.

When they reached the Crandals' they took off their ponies' tack, wiped them down, gave them some water, and let them out to graze. You are lucky ponies, thought Pam. Ginger is alone in a dark, dirty shed.

"Let's go up to the barn loft and go over our evidence," suggested Lulu.

The three girls climbed the ladder to the loft and sat around their hay bale table. Anna opened her drawing pad and put it in

front of Pam and Lulu. "This is a drawing of the inside of Ginger's shed," she explained.

"This shed is in terrible shape," said Anna. "The poop hasn't been cleaned up in a long time. It smells really awful. And there were flies everywhere."

"Your drawing is a good piece of

evidence," said Pam.

"What evidence do you have, Lulu?" asked Anna.

Lulu read her notes about Ginger out loud.

Ginger is an old pony.

It is a beautiful day, but Ginger is inside.

Ginger limps.

"I could tell she's old because she has a very swayed back," said Lulu.

"I noticed that, too," said Anna.

"How could you tell that she's lame?" asked Pam.

"I walked her in a circle," explained Lulu. "She didn't like to put weight on her back legs."

"She probably needs more exercise," said Pam.

"What is your evidence?" Lulu asked Pam.

Pam handed her notes to Lulu. Lulu read them out loud.

Ginger's hooves are cracked and overgrown.

Her coat is dirty and matted.

She is too thin.

"Those overgrown hooves could be making her limp," said Pam.

"But why is Ginger so thin?" asked Lulu. "There's feed on the floor. The mice haven't eaten all of it."

Pam thought for a minute. "Maybe the feed has gone bad," she said. Pam took out her pencil to add "bad feed" to her list.

Lulu put her hand on Pam's arm. "Don't write that down yet," she said. "We don't know for sure if the feed has gone bad. We should only put down what we know for certain."

"You're right," agreed Pam.

"So, what are we going to do for Ginger?" asked Lulu.

"Maybe we should call the police," said Anna.

Lulu pointed to the drawing and the notes. "We have plenty of evidence."

"I think we need more evidence," said Pam. "Animal abuse is a serious charge."

"Let's ask your father if he knows Ginger," said Lulu. "Maybe he's taken care of her."

"My dad is away at a veterinary conference," said Pam. "He won't be home for two days."

"Two days!" exclaimed Anna. "Ginger could be dead in two days."

"I think we should call the police right away," said Lulu.

"I already told you," Pam said. "I think we need more evidence."

"You saw Ginger," said Lulu. "You know she's in trouble, Pam. I don't understand why you don't want to report animal abuse."

"I want to visit Ginger one more time," insisted Pam.

"But Anna and I think we should report those awful people today," said Lulu.

Anna held up two fingers. "It's two against one, Pam. That means we do what

Lulu and I want."

Pam wanted to scream, "I know more about ponies than you do. You have to do what I want." Instead she said, "Please, let's go back to see Ginger tomorrow morning. We'll bring her fresh oats and clean out her shed."

Anna and Lulu exchanged a glance.

"Okay," said Anna.

"We'll go there one more time," added Lulu, "but then we report those people to the police."

Pam thought about the old man limping towards the run-down house. He had holes in his sweater. The old woman had a sad look on her face. Who were these people? Why weren't they taking better care of their pony?

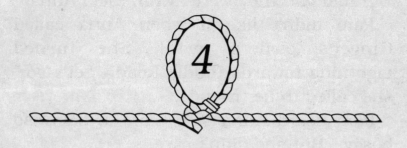

Pony Thieves

The next morning Pam put fresh feed and hay in Lightning's saddle bags. She rode Lightning into the field and waited for Lulu and Anna to ride out of Pony Pal Trail. When Pam finally saw her friends, she rode over to meet them.

"I spoke on the phone with my dad last night," Pam told them. "He doesn't know anything about Ginger or the people who own her."

"They don't even have a vet to take care of their pony!" exclaimed Lulu.

"I told you they were awful," said Anna.

Pam didn't like it when Anna called Ginger's owners awful. She turned Lightning towards Riddle Road. "Let's go," she called to her friends.

Pam heard Anna say, "Pam is being so bossy." But she didn't care.

When the Pony Pals reached the woods they dismounted and walked their ponies to the edge of the field. "I'll stay with our ponies," offered Lulu. "You two can take care of Ginger."

Lulu slung the saddle bags over her shoulder. Lightning nickered as if to say, "I want to go with you."

"You stay here," Pam told her pony. "I'll be right back."

Pam and Anna ran across the field to Ginger's shed. The old pony whinnied when she saw them.

"We have a lot to do," Pam told Anna. "You fill the water bucket and I'll start to groom her."

"Yes, boss," mumbled Anna.

Pam went into Ginger's shed. It smelt horrible. We should take Ginger outside while we clean this mess, she thought. She found a halter on the floor and slipped it over Ginger's head.

When Anna came in with the bucket of water, Pam told her to take it back out. "I'm bringing Ginger outside. You watch the house," she said to Anna.

Anna glared at Pam and left.

Pam hated it when she and Anna fought. "My friends are angry with me," Pam told the pony. "But I don't think your owners are awful people. I just don't."

She pulled on the halter to turn Ginger around. "Time for some fresh air and a good grooming," she told her. Pam stuck her head out the door.

"All clear," Anna told her.

Pam led Ginger out of the shed. The pony lowered her head and drank from the bucket. Pam opened one of the saddle bags. She held out a handful of hay. Ginger sniffed it and turned away.

"What's wrong?" Pam asked. "Aren't you hungry?"

Pam offered the pony a handful of grain. Ginger's soft lips brushed against Pam's outstretched hand. She took a mouthful of grain, chewed it a little, and spat it out.

"Why aren't you eating?" asked Pam.

Suddenly Ginger whinnied and backed away. In the same instant Pam saw Lightning charging across the field towards her. Ginger ran and limped towards Lightning.

Pam tried to catch the ponies. But even Ginger was faster than she was.

"Anna," Pam yelled, "help me."

Anna came running into the field and the two girls tried to corner the ponies. Finally, Ginger stopped. Then Lightning stopped. She walked over to Ginger and sniffed noses with her new friend.

Pam grabbed Ginger's halter and Anna took Lightning's reins. Both girls were breathless from chasing the ponies.

"You take Lightning," said Pam. "I'll put

Ginger back in the shed. We'd better get out of here."

Lightning whinnied loudly as if to say, "I don't want to go. I want to stay with my new friend."

"Come on," Anna told Lightning in a firm voice, "we have to go." She turned Lightning around and ran with her towards the woods.

The old pony was tired from running, so Pam had to lead her slowly towards the shed. Pam's heart pounded. Was the old couple home? Did they hear the noise? Did they see the ponies running through the fields?

"Pam, watch out!" yelled Anna.

Pam turned quickly and saw Ginger's owners coming across the field towards her.

"Stop, thieves!" the man yelled. He was swinging something over his head. It looked like a shotgun.

Pam dropped Ginger's lead and ran towards the woods.

She could run faster than the man and woman. In a minute she and Lightning were following their Pony Pals through the woods.

When the Pony Pals reached Mudge Road Extension they mounted their ponies and rode towards town. They didn't stop until they were at the corner of Main Street and Mudge Road.

"Let's go right to the police," said Lulu.

"That man and woman are probably calling the police about us," said Pam. "We were trespassing."

"You still don't want to turn them in!" challenged Anna.

"No, I don't," said Pam. "I think we should find out more about Ginger's owners. We need to figure out why they are neglecting their pony."

"They're horrible people," said Anna. "That's why they abuse Ginger."

"He was pointing a gun at you," said Lulu. "He wanted to shoot you."

"It wasn't a gun," said Pam. "It looked

like a gun. But it was a cane. That means he probably has trouble walking."

The Pony Pals led their ponies along Main Street.

"I thought it was a gun," said Anna.

"Well, it wasn't," said Pam. "I'm sure about that."

"Pam, why don't you want to tell the police about Ginger's owners?" asked Lulu.

"We don't know anything about that old couple," explained Pam. "They might need help, too."

Pam looked at Anna and Lulu. Would they agree with her? Or would there be a big Pony Pal fight?

Anna thought for a few seconds and nodded. "Maybe you're right," she said.

"We don't even know their names," said Lulu. "There's a lot we don't know about them."

"I'm sorry I was so bossy," Pam said.

"I hate it when you act like that," said Anna.

"I know," said Pam. "I hate it, too."

Anna put her hand on Pam's shoulder. "We forgive you."

"Thanks," said Pam.

"So how are we going to find out about Ginger's owners?" asked Lulu.

"Let's start at Town Hall," suggested Pam. "The town clerk will tell us who lives on that property."

The Pony Pals put their ponies in Acorn's and Snow White's paddock and walked over to Town Hall.

A young woman stood at a counter in the front office. "Hello, girls," she said. "What can I do for you?"

Pam described the property where they found Ginger.

The woman took out a big book and opened it in the middle. She turned a few pages. "Here it is," she said. "Richard and Gertrude Quinn. They have owned that property off Mudge Road Extension for seventy years."

"Seventy years!" exclaimed Anna. "That's a long time."

"It certainly is," said the clerk. "I'm surprised that they're still alive."

Pam wrote in her notebook.

Richard and Gertrude Quinn.
Have lived on farm for seventy years.

Where do we go next, wondered Pam. Who can tell us about Richard and Gertrude Quinn? And what will we learn?

Milk and Eggs

"Do you know Mr. and Mrs. Quinn?" Lulu asked the town clerk.

"No," she answered, "but I've only lived in Wiggins a few years."

The Pony Pals thanked the town clerk and went back outside.

"Who would know the Quinns?" asked Pam.

"We should ask someone who has lived in Wiggins all their lives," said Anna.

"Like my grandmother," suggested Lulu. "She knows everybody in Wiggins. She was born here."

The Pony Pals ran all the way to Grandmother Sanders's beauty parlor. She was cutting the curly hair of a red-headed woman.

The Pony Pals said hello to Grandmother Sanders. She introduced them to the red-headed woman. Her name was Shirley.

"We need your help, Grandma," said Lulu.

"Would you like some curls?" Grandmother asked with a smile. "I would love to curl that straight hair of yours, Lulu."

"I don't need curls," Lulu said. "We need information."

"We're trying to find out about some people," said Anna. "We thought you might know them."

Pam opened her notebook. "Their names are Richard and Gertrude Quinn," she said. "They live off Mudge Road Extension."

"Richard Quinn," said Shirley. "I haven't thought of him in years. Is he still alive?"

"Yes," said Anna. "His wife is, too."

"Quinn," said Grandmother thoughtfully. She put down the scissors.

"You remember Richard Quinn," Shirley told Lulu's grandmother. "He drove a pony cart through town every day when I was a kid. He parked near the Town Green. We bought his milk and eggs."

"I remember that," said Grandmother. "Quinn's Milk and Eggs. Those were the best eggs I've ever had. And good, sweet milk."

"Was Mr. Quinn a nice person?" asked Lulu.

"Oh my, yes," said Grandmother. "He was always smiling."

"He had a cute pony pulling that milk cart," said Shirley. "And a cat would ride with them. Remember that black cat, Lucinda?"

"I do indeed," said Grandmother. She took the cape off Shirley's shoulders and clippings of red hair fell to the floor.

Pam wrote:

Sold milk and eggs from cart.

Black cat in cart.

"Was the pony's name Ginger?" asked Pam.

"Ginger," repeated Shirley. "I do believe that's it."

"We saw Ginger," said Anna. "She's very old."

"She would be," said Shirley. "I'm remembering that pony from thirty years ago."

The Pony Pals thanked Grandmother Sanders and Shirley and went back to the kitchen.

"What do we do next?" asked Anna.

"I think we should investigate the Quinns," said Pam.

"You mean *spy* on them?" asked Lulu.

Pam nodded. "We should find out if they need help, too," she said. "It's important to our case."

"I totally agree with you," said Lulu.

"Me, too," added Anna. She raised three fingers. "It's three against zero."

Pam was glad they all agreed about what to do next.

The girls went out to the paddock behind Anna's house. They saddled up their ponies and rode out to the Quinns'. At the Quinns' they hitched their ponies to the trees.

Pam stayed with the ponies while Lulu and Anna went to peek through the windows of the farmhouse.

Fifteen minutes later Anna returned.

"What did you see?" asked Pam.

"There's an old dog," said Anna. "Mr. Quinn yells at him all the time."

"What about Mr. and Mrs. Quinn?" asked Pam.

"They're really old," said Anna. "Mrs. Quinn yells at Mr. Quinn. The house is very dirty."

"It sounds awful," said Pam. "Where's Lulu?"

"She's still there," said Anna. "I'll watch

the ponies. You can see for yourself."

Pam sneaked along the edge of the woods. She crouched down to run across the overgrown lawn to the house. Lulu was looking in a back window. Pam stood beside her.

Inside, the house was dark. Pam noticed that there were no lights on in the house. Was the Quinns' electricity turned off because they didn't pay the bill? Were they that poor?

Pam saw Mrs. Quinn put something on the table. It looked like crackers and a wrinkled apple.

"Come on and eat this," Pam heard Mrs. Quinn yell. Mr. Quinn didn't move. Mrs. Quinn yelled louder. This time Mr. Quinn heard her. He stood up and limped over to the table.

Mr. Quinn can't hear, Pam realized. That's why they yell.

Mr. Quinn sat at the table. "That's the end of the crackers," shouted Mrs. Quinn.

"You eat these," Mr. Quinn said in a loud

voice. He handed his wife two crackers. Then he bent over and patted the dog. He gave the dog the last cracker. "Here, Snappy," he said.

Pam's throat tightened and tears filled her eyes. These poor people, she thought. They don't have enough food. They need help as much as Ginger.

What could the Pony Pals do to help the Quinns, their dog, and their old pony?

Three Ideas

The Pony Pals rode quickly back towards Pam's place. The sun was low in the sky. They stopped when they reached the Crandals' big field.

"Anna and I had better keep going," Lulu told Pam. "We have to be home before dark."

"What are we going to do about Ginger and the Quinns?" asked Anna.

"We should all think of solutions to this problem tonight," suggested Pam.

"We can have a Pony Pal breakfast

meeting at the diner tomorrow," Anna said. Anna's mother owned the Off Main diner. It was a perfect place for Pony Pal meetings.

"Let's meet there at nine o'clock," said Lulu.

Pam watched her friends gallop across the field towards Pony Pal Trail. She brought Lightning into the barn, took off her tack and wiped her down. Taking care of a pony is hard work, she thought. Mr. and Mrs. Quinn were old and probably sick. No wonder they couldn't take good care of Ginger.

The next morning Pam rode Lightning to the diner. Snow White and Acorn were already at the hitching post. Pam tied Lightning beside them and went inside.

Anna and Lulu were waiting for Pam in their favorite booth. "We both want orange juice and French toast," said Lulu. "What about you?"

"I'll have the same thing," said Pam.

Lulu gave the cook their order. Anna went to the counter and poured three

glasses of orange juice. Pam set the table.
When they were all back at the booth they
began their Pony Pal Meeting.

"We have to find ways to help Mr. and
Mrs. Quinn," said Lulu.

"I forgot about the dog," said Pam.

"We should help the Quinns take care of
Ginger," said Anna.

"That's a good idea," Lulu said. "But they

won't let us do that. They think we're pony thieves."

"We have to make friends with them," suggested Anna.

"That's where my idea comes in," said Lulu. She read her idea out loud.

Write a letter to the Quinns. Tell them we are sorry that we trespassed on their land and scared them.

"That's a great idea," Pam said. "The letter could say we want to help Ginger."

"The Quinns need help, too," said Lulu. "They don't have electricity or enough food."

"That's where my idea comes in," Pam said. She read her idea to Lulu and Anna.

We should tell Ella Clark about the Quinns.

"Who is Ella Clark?" asked Lulu.

"She's the social worker for Wiggins," said Anna. "Her office is in Town Hall."

"Social workers help people," Pam told Lulu. "Ms. Clark is a friend of my mother's. She's very kind."

Anna's mother came to the booth with three plates of French toast.

"Thank you, Mrs. Harley," Lulu said.

"We forgot all about our food," said Pam. "We're working on a Pony Pal Problem."

Mrs. Harley put a plate in front of each girl and sat down beside Anna. "What's the problem this time?" she asked.

Anna told her mother about the Quinns.

"I remember them," said Mrs. Harley. "They were the sweetest people. And so generous. If there was a family going through hard times, the Quinns would leave free milk and eggs on their porch."

"That's so nice," said Lulu.

"My father died when I was your age,"

Mrs. Harley told the girls. "My mother had three children to raise on her own. Those were hard times for us. The Quinns often left milk and eggs on our porch. But they never gave my mother a bill."

"Now they are the ones having a hard time," Lulu said.

"I'd like you to take some food to them," said Mrs. Harley. "I'll make up a package right now." She stood up and went to the kitchen.

"We can deliver the letter when we take the food," suggested Anna.

"But the Quinns will recognize us," said Lulu. "They'll be angry and frightened when they see us."

"Let's take our ponies to the door," suggested Anna. "I bet they love ponies, especially Mr. Quinn. And we'll be very friendly."

The Pony Pals finished eating and cleared the table. Pam opened her notebook. "It's time to write our letter of apology," she said.

Dear Mr. and Mrs. Quinn,

Our names are Pam Crandal, Anna Harley and Lulu Sanders. We are sorry that we went on your land without permission. We are not pony thieves. We love ponies and would not hurt one. Ever. Pam's pony wanted to visit your pony. We all like Ginger. Could we help you take care of her? The food is a present for you from Anna's mother. You helped out her family many years ago. She wanted to say thank you.

Please forgive us for trespassing. We want to be your friends.

Sincerely,

Pam

Anna.

LULU

"That's a perfect letter," said Anna.

"I hope they'll like it," added Lulu.

Mrs. Harley brought three bags to the booth. "I've packed soup, two loaves of bread, some meat loaf with mashed potatoes, string beans and brownies," she said. "Tell them to come into the diner for a free meal anytime they want. Tell them that I want to pay them back for helping my family."

"Thanks, Mom," said Anna.

The Pony Pals put the food in their saddle bags and rode back to the Quinns'. Anna and Lulu were in a good mood, but Pam was nervous. What if the Quinns were afraid of them? What if they weren't nice people anymore?

Dear Mr. and Mrs. Quinn

The Pony Pals rode up the dirt driveway to the Quinns' house. They got off their ponies and took the packages of food out of their saddle bags. Pam knocked on the front door. All three girls smiled at Mrs. Quinn when she opened it. Mrs. Quinn looked surprised to see them.

"Hello," said Anna. She held out the letter. "This is for you."

"Who's there?" Mr. Quinn yelled from the living room.

"Three girls!" yelled Mrs. Quinn. "With

ponies!"

Mrs. Quinn took the letter. She was studying the girls and their ponies. A frightened look came over her face. She stepped back. "You are the girls who tried to steal Ginger," she said.

"We weren't stealing Ginger," said Lulu. "We were visiting her. We're sorry that we scared you."

Pam could hear the tap tap of Mr. Quinn's cane as he crossed the living room. He came into the hall and saw the Pony Pals at the door. An angry look came over his face. "The pony thieves," he shouted.

Mrs. Quinn put her hand on his arm. "Just children, Richard," she said.

Pam thought Mr. Quinn was the oldest looking man that she had ever seen.

"Please read the letter," Lulu said.

Mrs. Quinn opened the envelope and held it up so her husband could read it, too.

When they finished reading, Mrs. Quinn looked up at the Pony Pals. "You like

Ginger," she said. "Children have always loved Ginger."

"She's a sweet pony," said Anna. "We wondered if we could groom her for you."

Mrs. Quinn looked at the ponies behind the girls. "You have your own ponies," she said.

"We love all ponies," Lulu said.

"It's hard work to take care of a pony," added Pam. "We want to help you."

"I'm Anna Harley," Anna told Mr. Quinn in a loud voice. "My grandmother's name was Violet Croft. You helped her after her husband died."

"Croft," said Mr. Quinn. "Her husband died in an automobile crash."

Anna held up a bag of food. "My mother owns a diner. She sent you some food as a thankyou present."

"Can we put it in the kitchen for you?" asked Pam.

"You helped Mrs. Croft," Mrs. Quinn said to her husband. "I think we should accept her gift."

Mr. Quinn nodded.

"I'll stay with our ponies," said Lulu.

Pam and Anna followed the Quinns into the kitchen. They put the bags of food on the table.

"Can we see Ginger now?" asked Pam in a loud voice.

"They're good children," Mrs. Quinn shouted to her husband. "And Ginger has been lonely."

Mr. Quinn thought for a moment. "Yes. Okay."

Anna and Pam went back out front. The girls led their ponies towards Ginger's shed. Ginger whinnied a hello and Lightning answered her with a happy nicker.

Anna and Lulu put their ponies and Lightning in the fenced-in field near Ginger's shed. Pam opened the door to the shed and led Ginger out in the small paddock. The pony lay her head on Pam's shoulder. Pam patted her. "We're going to take care of you," she said.

Lulu gave Ginger a bucket of water. When she drank all she wanted, Pam offered her some hay. She took a bite, chewed it and spat it out.

"Let's try some grain," said Pam. She went into the shed. She put a handful of feed in a bucket and brought it outside. Pam looked at the feed closely. "It's not moldy," she told Pam and Lulu. She smelt it. "It smells okay." Next she crushed the grains between her fingers. "And it feels fresh."

Lulu held out the bucket for Ginger. The old pony put her nose in the bucket and sniffed. But she didn't eat any of it.

"I wonder why she isn't eating?" said Pam.

"Maybe she's sick," suggested Anna.

"When is your father coming home, Pam?" asked Lulu.

"This afternoon," replied Pam.

"Maybe he can tell us what's wrong with her," suggested Anna.

"If the Quinns will let him look at her,"

said Pam. "I'll ask Mrs. Quinn."

"Let's clean out the shed first," suggested Lulu.

The girls went into the shed. "The mice certainly like the feed," said Anna. "They've made a mess in here."

When they finished shoveling and sweeping out the shed, the Pony Pals put clean straw on the floor. They were grooming Ginger when Mrs. Quinn came up to them. She was smiling. She handed an envelope to Anna. "Give this to your mother. It's our thankyou note for the wonderful food. That meat loaf was delicious."

"My mom said you should come to the diner for a meal whenever you want," said Anna. "It's her way to pay you back for the free milk and eggs."

"We don't have a car anymore," said Mrs. Quinn. "We can't manage a pony cart. Ginger can't either."

No wonder we never see them in town, thought Pam. They don't have any way to get there.

"How do you shop and go to the doctor?" asked Lulu.

"We don't need much. And we have a friend who helps us out a little," she said. "But poor Mildred isn't doing so well herself these days." Mrs. Quinn sighed.

"There's a social worker in Wiggins," said Anna. "She could help you."

"We don't like to have visitors," said Mrs. Quinn.

"Why not?" blurted out Anna.

"Mr. Quinn is afraid they will put us in a home for old people," she said. "Then what would happen to Ginger and Snappy? No one wants useless, old animals. They would be put to sleep. That is why we don't want visitors."

No visitors, thought Pam. Then how can we help the Quinns?

Four Riders

Mrs. Quinn admired the clean shed. "Thank you, girls," she said. "Now it will be easier for me to keep it clean." She patted Ginger's side. "And Ginger looks lovely without her winter coat."

"The mice have been making a mess of the shed," said Anna. "They chewed open the feed bags."

"Mice are a problem since our cat, Toby, died," said Mrs. Quinn. "Toby was a wonderful mouser and a wonderful cat." She patted Ginger's side again. "Wasn't he, Ginger?"

Lulu held another handful of feed out for Ginger. The pony took a mouthful of grain, tried to chew it, and spat it out.

"I wonder why she doesn't keep chewing," said Lulu. "She has a lot of teeth."

Pam suddenly had an idea. She put a hand on Ginger's lip and pushed it up. Pam looked inside her mouth. "Her teeth might be too long," she said. "That happens with ponies, especially old ponies. Then they can't chew their food. Ginger's teeth should be filed down."

"Can your father do that?" Lulu asked Pam.

"Yes," said Pam. "And don't worry, it doesn't hurt." Pam rubbed her hands along Ginger's back legs. "I think she has arthritis, too. Maybe that's why she limps. My father has a medicine that would make it easier for her to walk."

"You should be a veterinarian," Mrs. Quinn told Pam.

"I will be some day," said Pam. "My father

is a vet. Sometimes I help him in his animal hospital. But I can't file teeth or prescribe medicines."

"Pam's father is an excellent vet," said Anna. "He takes good care of our ponies."

"He makes barn calls," added Pam. "He could give Ginger a check-up."

"It was very nice of you girls to come," said Mrs. Quinn. "But we don't want any more visitors."

Ginger sniffed the oats again, but didn't even try to eat. "I didn't know she wasn't eating," Mrs. Quinn said. She ran her hand along Ginger's side. "She *has* lost weight."

"*Please* let us bring Dr. Crandal here," said Anna.

Mrs. Quinn thought for a few seconds. "If he doesn't mind," she said at last. "I *would* like him to look at Ginger."

The Pony Pals said goodbye to Mrs. Quinn and rode back to the Crandals'. They put their ponies in the paddock and ran over to Dr. Crandal's office. He was giving shots to a big labrador retriever.

"We need to talk to you, Dad," said Pam.

"Hi, girls," he said. "I'll be right with you."

The girls went to the waiting room and sat down. Pam counted three people with dogs and two with cats. They were all waiting to see her father.

"I hope he isn't too busy to help Ginger," said Lulu.

"Oh, he'll help," assured Pam.

Dr. Crandal took care of two more patients, then he called the girls into his office.

"What's up?" he asked.

Pam told him about the Quinns, Ginger and Snappy.

"I'd be happy to see them," Dr. Crandal said. He went to the door and counted the animals in the waiting room. Then he looked at his watch. "I'll be finished here in an hour," he said. "I'd like to ride over to the Quinns' with you. I haven't exercised J.B. in over a week. Could you girls saddle him up for me?"

The Pony Pals said they would have J.B.

and their three ponies ready for the ride to the Quinns'.

J.B. was Dr. Crandal's palamino thoroughbred horse. The Pony Pals admired J.B. It would be fun to groom him and put on Dr. Crandal's black western saddle. They went over to the new barn to find the big horse. An hour later Dr. Crandal and the Pony Pals rode over to the Quinns'. Dr. Crandal had his veterinary bag roped to the back of his saddle.

Mr. and Mrs. Quinn were sitting on the porch with Snappy. They saw the four riders and waved.

Pam and her father rode up to the house side by side. "You have to shout when you talk to Mr. Quinn," she told her dad. "He's very hard of hearing."

Dr. Crandal gave Snappy a physical examination. "He's blind," Dr. Crandal told the Quinns. "But he seems to be doing okay. He knows his way around here." Next, Dr. Crandal moved his hands gently up and down the dog's legs. "Arthritis," he said. "We have pills that will help him with that."

Pam patted the old dog on the head. "You'll feel much better, Snappy," she said.

Dr. Crandal gave Snappy a dog biscuit and handed Mrs. Quinn a container of pills. He closed his doctor's bag. "Now let's take a look at this pony I've heard so much about," he said.

Lulu and Anna tied the three ponies and J.B. to the fence. Pam walked with her father and the Quinns over to Ginger's shed. Pam wondered if she was right. Were Ginger's teeth too long? Or was something more serious keeping her from eating?

Ginger was happy to be led out of her shed. She stood still and let Dr. Crandal examine her. "She's a very good patient," he said.

"She's thirty-five years old," Mrs. Quinn told Dr. Crandal. "And she doesn't like to eat anymore."

"My daughter is right," Dr. Crandal told the Quinns. "Ginger's teeth look too long.

I'll file them down. Then we'll see if she'll eat."

Dr. Crandal took two long files out of his black bag. "One is for the upper teeth," Dr. Crandal explained. "The other one is for the lower teeth."

When Dr. Crandal finished filing Ginger's teeth, Lulu held up a handful of hay. Ginger grabbed it with her mouth and chewed. This time she didn't spit out the hay half-chewed. She chewed some more and swallowed it. She snorted as if to say, "This is much better."

Everyone laughed.

Next Dr. Crandal walked Ginger around and ran his hands over her legs. "She has arthritis," he told the Quinns.

"Your daughter said the same thing," said Mrs. Quinn. "She said there is a new medicine for that."

Dr. Crandal put a hand on Pam's shoulder. "She's right," he said smiling. "My daughter, the vet."

"What about Ginger's hooves?" Pam

asked her dad.

"They should be trimmed," he said. "Those overgrown hooves are also making it difficult for her to walk." He turned to Mr. Quinn and said in a loud voice. "I can send the ferrier over here."

"I used to trim Ginger's hooves myself," said Mr. Quinn. "But I can't bend over to do it now."

"Mr. Conway is very good," Pam told Mr. Quinn. "He takes care of our ponies."

"Yes, yes," said Mr. Quinn. "I know Conway. He'll do a good job."

Dr. Crandal and the Pony Pals said goodbye to Mr. and Mrs. Quinn. Pam went over to Ginger and rubbed her nose. "Bye, Ginger," she said. "I hope we'll see you soon." She looked deep into Ginger's eyes. You're still sad, thought Pam. You're groomed and you can eat again. But you're still the saddest pony I've ever seen.

That night the Pony Pals had a barn sleep-over in the barn loft. After they said goodnight to their ponies, they climbed the ladder to the loft. They laid their sleeping bags out in a row facing the open window. Through the window Pam saw a bright star beside a full moon.

"Star bright, star bright," said Pam.

Anna and Lulu joined in. The Pony Pals completed the poem together.

"The first star I see tonight.

I wish I may.

I wish I might.

Have the wish I wish tonight."

"Now make a wish," whispered Anna. The three girls were quiet for a few seconds.

"What did you wish?" asked Lulu.

"I wished that the Quinns could have electricity and more food," said Anna.

"I wished that Ella Clark will help them," said Lulu.

"And I wished that I could make Ginger happier," said Pam.

"Those are all good wishes," said Anna.

Pam stared at the lone star and thought hard, *please*, make our wishes come true.

Fat Cat's Kitten

The next morning after breakfast the Pony Pals rode to town. They left their ponies in the paddock and went over to Town Hall. Pam led the way up the stairs to Ella Clark's office. The door to the social services office was open. Ms. Clark was sitting at her desk. She saw the Pony Pals and invited them in. "What can I do for you girls?" she asked.

Pam told Ms. Clark about the Quinns.

"We wondered if you can help them," Lulu said.

"I'm certain that we can," said Ms. Clark.

"But Mr. and Mrs. Quinn don't want to move from their house," Pam explained.

"They want to stay with their animals," said Lulu. "They don't want to move to a nursing home."

"It's very important to them," added Anna.

"They should be able to stay in their own house," said Ms. Clark. "We can help them right there."

"How?" asked Lulu.

"I can enroll them in Meals on Wheels," Ms. Clark answered.

"What's that?" asked Pam.

"Someone will drive to their house every day," Ms. Clark explained. "And bring them a hot meal."

"That would be a big help," said Anna.

"We can also take them to the doctor," said Ms. Clark. "We have a lot of services for people like the Quinns." Ella Clark looked at her watch. "I can go see them right now," she said. "And be back in time for my next appointment." She smiled at the Pony Pals. "I'm glad you girls found the Quinns."

"My pony, Lightning, found them," said Pam. "She's good at finding animals and people who need help."

"Well, thank Lightning for me," said Ms. Clark.

The Pony Pals said goodbye to Ella Clark and left Town Hall.

A few minutes later the three girls were sitting on the paddock fence watching their ponies. Snow White was pulling hay from the hay net. Lightning was asleep under the tree. Acorn was standing near the shed watching his cat, Shadow, asleep on a hay bale.

"I'm worried," said Pam.

"About what?" asked Anna.

"That the Quinns will be angry at us for talking to the social worker," answered Pam. "They said they don't want any more visitors. Now Ella Clark is going to visit them. And it's our fault."

"We did it to help them," said Lulu.

"I know," said Pam. "But maybe they won't let us visit Ginger anymore."

"Ginger is still so sad," said Lulu. "She needs friends."

Acorn lowered his head and pushed Shadow with his nose. The cat rolled on his back. Acorn nuzzled his belly.

"Shadow loves it when Acorn does that," said Anna.

"It's so cute," said Lulu.

"They're best friends," said Anna. "Acorn would be so sad if anything happened to Shadow."

Pam turned to Anna. "What did you say?" she asked.

"They're best friends," repeated Anna. "Acorn would be so sad if anything happened to Shadow."

"That's it," said Pam.

"What's what?" asked Lulu.

"Mrs. Quinn said that they had a cat that died recently," said Pam.

"A cat named Toby," remembered Lulu.

"Maybe Ginger is sad because she misses the cat," Pam said.

"The woman at your grandmother's beauty parlor said there was always a cat in the Quinn's pony cart," said Lulu.

"I bet Ginger always had a cat," added Anna.

"Let's give Ginger another cat," suggested Pam. "Maybe then she won't be so sad."

"A cat would also chase the mice out of Ginger's shed," said Lulu. "That would be a big help to the Quinns."

"Where do we get a cat?" asked Anna.

"I still have one of Fat Cat's kittens," said Pam excitedly. "He's turning into a good mouser."

"Of course, the black-and-white one we named Pal," said Lulu.

"Pal is adorable," Anna said. "But I thought you wanted to keep him, Pam."

"I did," said Pam. "But we have plenty of cats on the farm. The Quinns don't have any. Besides, my mother said I should try to find a home for Pal."

The Pony Pals quickly saddled up their ponies and rode on Pony Pal Trail to Pam's. They found little Pal in the tack room. He was lying on the floor next to the feed box. When he saw the Pony Pals he ran over to them and climbed up Pam's leg. Pam picked up the kitten and held him in her arms.

"Listen to him purr," said Anna. "He's such a sweet kitten."

Pam fluffed up Pal's shiny black coat. He licked her hand.

Anna's right, thought Pam. You are sweet.

"Maybe you should keep him and find Ginger another kitten," said Lulu.

Pam looked into Pal's green eyes. She didn't want to give the sweet kitten away. But she knew he would be a good mouser for the Quinns. And a good stable mate for Ginger.

The Pony Pals went to the new barn to find Mrs. Crandal. She was saddling up a school pony for a riding student. Pam told her mother that they had found a home for the black-and-white kitten.

"Good," said Mrs. Crandal. "Now we've found homes for all of Fat Cat's kittens. How are you going to get him over to the Quinns'?"

"I'll put him in the soft cat carrier," Pam said. "And stick the carrier in front of me on the saddle."

"That should work if you're riding Lightning," said Mrs. Crandal. She smiled. "I've never seen a pony who loved other animals as much as Lightning."

The Pony Pals went back to the old barn to look for the cat carrier.

"I hope Ginger likes Pal," said Pam.

"And Pal likes Ginger," Lulu said.

"I hope the Quinns still like us," added Anna.

Pam felt a worry-knot in her chest. What if the Quinns were mad at the Pony Pals for telling a social worker about them? What if they wouldn't let Ella Clark help them?

Up a Tree

Pam found the cat carrier in the tack room closet. She saddled up Lightning. Next, she put Pal in the carrier. "You're going to a new home today, Pal." She zipped the carrier closed. "I'll miss you. But Lightning and I will visit."

Anna held the cat carrier while Pam mounted Lightning.

"We have a passenger today," Pam told her pony.

Anna handed Pam the carrier. Pal meowed and moved around in the carrier. But

Lightning didn't spook. She whinnied gently as if to say, "Don't worry, kitty. You are safe with me."

Lulu and Anna mounted their ponies and rode across the field to Riddle Road. When they reached the Quinns' they rode up to the house.

No one was on the front porch. No one came out to greet them.

"Maybe they're in the kitchen and didn't hear us," said Pam.

Lulu jumped off Snow White and went up to the front door. She knocked loudly.

No one answered.

"They might be in the barn or with Ginger," suggested Pam.

The girls led their ponies to the barn. Pam carried the cat carrier in one hand and led Lightning with the other. Pal meowed as if to say, "I want to get out of this carrier *now.*"

"I'll let you out in a minute," Pam told the kitten.

Lulu and Anna looked in the barn. Mr. and Mrs. Quinn weren't there.

They went to Ginger's shed. Ginger was there. But Mr. and Mrs. Quinn were not.

"I wonder where they are?" said Lulu in a worried voice.

Just then a car came up the driveway. The Pony Pals tied their ponies to the fence and ran over to the car.

The Quinns and Ella stood beside the car and waited for them. They were all smiling. Mr. and Mrs. Quinn aren't angry at us, thought Pam.

"Hello, girls," said Mrs. Quinn. "I'm glad you came to visit Ginger. She's still acting sad."

"We came to cheer her up," said Lulu.

"We were worried because you weren't here," Anna told Mrs. Quinn.

"I took the Quinns to the supermarket," Ms. Clark told the girls. "Now I have to get back to my office." She opened the car trunk. "Could you girls take the grocery bags out of my car?"

"Sure," said Anna.

Mr. Quinn pointed to Ella. "I knew her grandmother," he said. "Went to school with her grandmother."

Mrs. Quinn put a hand on Ella Clark's arm. "Ella is a dear," she said. "I didn't think we could stay on the farm. I thought we'd have to go to one of those homes for old people. But with Ella's help we can live in our own house."

Anna and Lulu took the groceries into the house. Mr. Quinn followed them in.

"He needs to rest," Mrs. Quinn told Pam.

Pal meowed and scratched at the door of his carrier.

"Do we have another visitor?" asked Mrs. Quinn.

"I hope he's a new friend for Ginger," said Pam. She unzipped the carrier and took out the kitten. "This is Pal," she told Mrs. Quinn. "He's a present from me."

"Ginger loves cats!" exclaimed Mrs. Quinn. She took Pal from Pam and held him to her chest. "I love cats, too." Pal purred. Mrs. Quinn looked at his face. "This is a sweet cat," she said.

"He is sweet," agreed Pam. "But he is also a good mouser."

"We could use a good mouser," Mrs. Quinn

said. "Let's bring him over to meet Ginger." She handed the kitten back to Pam. "You can introduce them."

Lulu and Anna came out of the house. The Pony Pals and Mrs. Quinn brought Pal over to Ginger's paddock. Ginger ran over to the fence to meet them.

"Ginger is hardly limping anymore," Lulu said.

"Thanks to Dr. Crandal's pills," said Mrs. Quinn.

Pam put Pal on the ground. Ginger lowered her head to sniff the kitten. Suddenly, Pal went up on his hind legs, swiped Ginger's nose with a paw, hissed, and ran up a nearby tree.

"I don't think Pal likes ponies," said Anna.

Pam felt disappointed. "Fat Cat likes ponies. I thought Pal would, too."

Ginger looked up at the tree limb and whinnied. Pal hissed and climbed to a higher limb on the tree. Ginger turned and walked away.

Pam went over to Ginger. "I'm sorry,

Ginger," she said. "I thought Pal liked ponies. His mother does." Pam looked into Ginger's eyes. They weren't sad anymore. It almost looked like Ginger was smiling.

Ginger gazed over her shoulder at the tree and nickered a low, deep sound. Pal stared at Ginger. But this time he didn't go higher in the tree. And he didn't hiss.

Mrs. Quinn came up beside Pam. "Ginger has a way with cats," she whispered. "He'll make friends with Pal. It might take time, but they will be friends."

"Maybe we should leave them alone for a while," said Lulu.

"Let's go back to the house," suggested Mrs. Quinn. "I bought cookies and milk for you girls. And some apples for the ponies."

The Pony Pals went back to the house with Mrs. Quinn. Mr. Quinn was sleeping in a chair in the living room. Snappy was curled up and asleep at his feet.

After the snack, the Pony Pals went back to the paddock. Pal wasn't in the paddock. Pam looked up in the tree. Pal wasn't there either.

"He's in here," yelled Anna. "In the shed."

"Chasing two mice!" added Lulu with a laugh.

Pam went to the window of the shed and looked in. There was Pal running two mice in circles.

Ginger came up next to Pam. She poked her head through the window and watched Pal chasing the mice, too. Ginger whinnied as if to say, "Good work, kitty."

Pal was too busy with the mice to even look at Ginger.

"Hey, mice," shouted Lulu, "you'd better give up and leave."

"This shed is for Ginger and her pal, Pal," Anna said.

Pam patted Ginger's cheek. "It looks like you have a good stable mate." Pam looked back at her own pony. Lightning was watching carefully from the fence.

Pam ran over to her pony. She threw her arms around Lightning's neck. "Thank you, Lightning," she said. "Thank you for finding Ginger."

Dear Reader:

I am having a lot of fun researching and writing books about the Pony Pals. I've met many interesting kids and adults who love ponies. And I've visited some wonderful ponies at homes, farms and riding schools.

Before writing Pony Pals I wrote fourteen novels for children and young adults. Four of these were honored by Children's Choice Awards.

I live in Sharon, Connecticut, with my husband, Lee, and our dog, Willie. Our daughter is all grown up and has her own apartment in New York City.

Besides writing novels I like to draw, paint, garden and swim. I didn't have a pony when I was growing up, but I have always loved them and dreamt about riding. Now I take riding lessons on a horse named Saz.

I like reading and writing about ponies as much as I do riding. Which proves to me that you don't have to ride a pony to love them. And you certainly don't need a pony to be a Pony Pal.

Happy Reading,

Jeanne Betancourt